Attack on Pearl Harbor

THE RANGER IN TIME SERIES

RANGER in TIME

Attack on Pearl Harbor

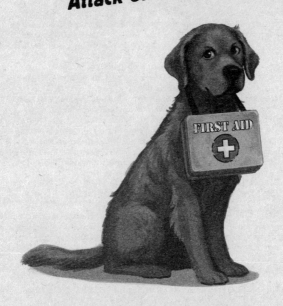

KATE MESSNER

illustrated by
KELLEY McMORRIS

Scholastic Inc.

Text copyright © 2020 by Kate Messner
Illustrations by Kelley McMorris, copyright © 2020 Scholastic Inc.

This book is being published simultaneously in hardcover by Scholastic Press.

Library of Congress Cataloging-in-Publication Data
Names: Messner, Kate, author. | McMorris, Kelley, illustrator. | Messner,
Kate. Ranger in time ; 12.
Title: Attack on Pearl Harbor / Kate Messner ; illustrated by Kelley McMorris.
Description: New York : Scholastic Inc., 2020. | Series: Ranger in time; book 12 | Includes bibliographical references. | Audience: Ages 7-10 |Audience: Grades 4-6 | Audience: Ages 7-10 | Audience: Grades 4-6 | Summary: This time Ranger, the time-travelling Golden retriever finds himself transported to the deck of the USS Arizona on December 7, 1941, where he rescues the young sailor Ben Hansen who is badly burned when the ship explodes — and there is a Japanese-American boy and girl in a rowboat who also need his help to find their father amid the chaos of the attack.
Identifiers: LCCN 2019022884 (print) | LCCN 2019022885 (ebook) |
ISBN 9781338537963 (trade paperback) | ISBN 9781338537970 (library binding) |
ISBN 9781338538144 (ebk)
Subjects: LCSH: Golden retriever — Juvenile fiction. | Pearl Harbor (Hawaii), Attack on, 1941 — Juvenile fiction. | Time travel — Juvenile fiction. | Rescues — Juvenile fiction. | Japanese Americans — Juvenile fiction. | Hawaii — History — 1900-1959 — Juvenile fiction. | CYAC: Golden retriever — Fiction. | Dogs — Fiction. | Pearl Harbor (Hawaii), Attack on, 1941 — Fiction. | Time travel — Fiction. | Rescues — Fiction. | Japanese Americans — Fiction. | Hawaii — History — 1900-1959 — Fiction. | LCGFT: Action and adventure fiction. | Historical fiction.
Classification: LCC PZ7.M5615 At 2020 (print) | LCC PZ7.M5615 (ebook) |
DDC 813.6 [Fic] — dc23
LC record available at https://lccn.loc.gov/2019022884

ISBN 978-1-338-53796-3

10 9 8 7 6 5 4 3 2 1   20 21 22 23 24

Printed in the U.S.A.   40
First printing 2020

Book design by Ellen Duda and Stephanie Yang

For Donna Macdonald and the readers of Orchard School

Chapter 1

READY FOR BATTLE

December 5, 1941

Ben Hansen looked out over the Hawaiian shoreline from the seat of a Kingfisher seaplane. Back home in Minnesota, December meant ice, snow, and air so cold it took your breath away. But here at Pearl Harbor, nearly every day was sunny. In less than a year, the island of Oahu had come to feel like home — but with much more pleasant weather!

Ben loved looking out at Pearl Harbor, where the US Navy's Pacific Fleet was stationed — more than a hundred vessels, including eight huge battleships. He loved the flurry of activity along the docks of Battleship Row. He loved the sparkling Pacific Ocean and the gentle winds that rustled the palm trees of nearby Waikiki Beach. That's where he'd spend his day off tomorrow.

For now, though, there was work to do. Ben checked his instruments and sent an update to the pilot in the front seat. Ben was a radio-man who flew scouting missions along with the Kingfisher pilots. They'd launch from their battleship, the USS *Arizona*, and soar over the Pacific.

It was Ben's job to navigate and communicate with the ship. He took care of all the electronics on the plane, too. When it was time to return to the USS *Arizona*, the seaplane would land in the waves and maneuver into position. Ben would need to grab a hook

dangling from the battleship's big crane, and he had to be fast! Sometimes, the waves threatened to tip him into the sea. But Ben was an expert with the hook. He'd snatch it out of the air and attach it to the plane so the crane could lift them back onto the ship.

Today, there was no need for that. The USS *Arizona* was in the harbor, so instead of landing at sea, the Kingfisher touched down on the runway at Ford Island.

"Got plans for your day of liberty tomorrow?" Ben asked Tom, the plane's pilot, as they headed back to the ship.

"Going into Honolulu to buy a Christmas gift for my girl back home," said Tom.

"I want to find something nice for my mother and sisters," Ben said. His two younger sisters lived with his mother, a librarian, back in St. Paul. They both had blond hair and freckles, like he did. Ben's father had died a long time ago, when he was very small, so his mother worked hard to take care of the family. As soon as he turned seventeen, Ben had signed up for the navy so he could help out. And he had to admit, he had done it for the travel, too. He'd always wanted to see some of the faraway places he'd read about in the stories his mother shared.

Each night before Ben went to sleep in his hammock, he'd take out a poem he kept tucked in his pocket. His mother had copied it onto a card for him and laminated it so it would last longer. The poem was from Ben's favorite book, *When We Were Very Young*. His mother had read it every night when he was growing up.

Little Boy kneels at the foot of the bed,
Droops on the little hands little gold head.
Hush! Hush! Whisper who dares!
Christopher Robin is saying his prayers.

Ben held the poem in his hands. The words, penned in his mother's handwriting, made her feel closer. He still read them to himself every night before he went to sleep.

After breakfast the next morning, Ben took a small boat to shore with some friends and caught a ride into town. It was December sixth — less than twenty days until Christmas! He couldn't decide on gifts for his family, but he bought some holiday cards to send home.

Ben and the other servicemen had lunch at the Black Cat Café. Ben brought along a rubber spider he'd picked up at the general store and dropped it on his friend Jerry's hamburger while he wasn't looking. The poor guy jumped about a mile when he saw it. But then he laughed.

"Every day is April Fools' Day when your name is Ben Hansen," Jerry said.

After lunch, Ben and his friends split up.

Jerry and Chow were in the USS *Arizona*'s band. Jerry was an ace at clarinet. Chow (short for Chowhound, because he loved to eat) was the best French horn player around. They wanted to be early for the Battle of Music, a competition of the ships' bands at Bloch Arena that night. Everyone would be there! But Ben and his other friends took a few more hours to enjoy the beach. They stretched out in the sand and rode the waves until the sun sank low in the sky.

They caught a ride back to Pearl Harbor in time to hear the bands. Ben didn't play an instrument, but he loved tapping his feet to the music. He hummed along to "There'll Be Some Changes Made" and "Georgia on My Mind." At the end of the night, he watched the jitterbug contest. A little girl who'd come to see the bands with her father stole the show, dancing with a sailor from the USS *Tennessee*.

It was after midnight when Ben returned to the ship and climbed into his hammock. He'd be back on duty in the morning. Even on free days, it was hard to forget the fleet's mission in Hawaii. President Roosevelt had sent them here because of threats from Japan. Some people were even saying the Japanese might attack the fleet!

The rumors made Ben wonder. The American navy was the best of the best. They were skilled. They were well trained. They were prepared for anything. Ben couldn't imagine the Japanese would dare to think about an attack. But if they did, he and his fellow servicemen would be ready.

Chapter 2

SYMBOL OF THE RISING SUN

December 7, 1941

Paul Yamada squinted into the sun as he pulled on the oars of his family's sixteen-foot rowboat. He made this trip every Sunday, bobbing over the waves of Pearl Harbor to Ford Island to sell eggs from the family's chickens. It was about a mile — a long way to row so early in the morning. Paul was twelve but strong for his age, and so was his twin sister, Grace. He was glad she'd come along to help today. Once they reached Ford Island, they'd load up the pushcart they kept at the dock and go door-to-door with their eggs.

The Yamada family grew vegetables and raised chickens in coops behind their house. It was a lot of work. Paul and Grace had an older sister named Helen who was busy learning to become a nurse, so the work of collecting eggs always fell to Paul and Grace. Each afternoon, they would pick the eggs from the coops, clean them, pack them into boxes, and deliver them to the market.

Paul and Grace's ojiichan, their grandfather, had been a farmer back in Japan, where he'd grown up. But farmers struggled there and had to pay high taxes. When he heard that immigrants were being hired in Hawaii, he made the journey across the sea to the island of Oahu.

There, he found work on a sugar plantation. He saved his money until he could build the small house where the Yamada family lived today. It was in a neighborhood with many other Japanese American families, including Paul's best friend, Jimmy Abe. Jimmy was always game to make stilts out of sticks to race Paul and Grace around the yard. When they were too tired to stilt-race anymore, they'd sit in the shade and read Captain America comic books. Paul's favorite was the one with Captain America punching Nazi leader Adolf Hitler on the cover.

Paul had heard all about the war in Europe on his father's radio. He knew that Hitler and the German army had invaded Poland two years ago, and were storming through the rest of Europe. Paul knew that Japan was also invading other nations. Just five months ago, Japan had seized Indochina. Lately, there had been whispers that Japan might attack the United States. Maybe even here in Hawaii!

He'd asked his grandmother, his obaachan, what she thought about that.

"Oh no," she said. "That will never, ever happen."

But Paul still thought about what he might do if it did. He wouldn't be afraid. He would run into the battle and save people. He'd be a hero, like Captain America.

Paul tugged harder on the oars. The mile to Ford Island felt extra long today. He wanted to get there and get his work done. If he and Grace could sell their eggs quickly, maybe he could ask Jimmy to bring over his latest Captain America comic that afternoon.

"Look!" Grace said, pointing to a couple of planes flying low over the mountains.

Paul stopped rowing for a moment to watch them. "The military must be doing exercises today."

"They're flying awfully low," Grace said.

Paul stared at the sky as the planes approached. They looked different from the ones that normally took off from Ford Island. And they *were* flying low. Too low.

As the first plane soared overhead, Paul caught a glimpse of red beneath its wing. He sucked in his breath. It was the Japanese maru, the symbol of the rising sun.

His grandmother was wrong. The worst thing he could imagine was happening. Japan had come to attack America. And it was happening *now*.

Chapter 3

DECK THE HALLS

"Come on, Ranger!" Luke called as he and Sadie jumped out of the car. Ranger bounded from the back seat into the snow. He was going with Luke and Sadie's family to choose a Christmas tree, like they did every December.

Ranger loved Christmas tree time. When they walked through the tree farm, Luke always threw snowballs for Ranger to catch. And when they went home, Sadie would sneak Ranger pieces of her Christmas cookies while Mom and Dad put up the tree.

"What do you think about this one,

Ranger?" Luke was pointing to a bushy pine tree when Ranger saw a flash of brown fur out of the corner of his eye.

Squirrel!

Ranger took off after it, bounding through the snow. He chased the squirrel between the trees and around a little shed. He chased the squirrel all the way to the edge of the woods until it disappeared up a very tall tree. It sat way up at the top, chattering down at him.

Ranger barked at the squirrel a few times. Then he ran back to Luke and Sadie.

"Guess you were more interested in that squirrel than our Christmas tree," Luke said, laughing.

It was true. Ranger loved chasing squirrels. That was the only reason he wasn't an official search-and-rescue dog.

Ranger had gone through all the search-and-rescue dog training with Luke and his dad. He'd learned to find missing people by following their scent. He'd practiced finding people in thick woods and grassy meadows. He'd practiced finding them in dark warehouses and fallen-down buildings. Ranger was very good at finding people and helping them.

But he wasn't good at ignoring squirrels. In order to be a search-and-rescue dog, you had to take a special test with lots of different challenges. You had to ignore everything except the people you were supposed to find. You had to ignore squeaky toys and juicy hot dog pieces in the grass. You also had to ignore squirrels.

Halfway through Ranger's test, a squirrel had run past. Ranger chased it.

If a real person had needed help that morning, Ranger would have left the squirrel alone and helped. But he knew that this was just a pretend rescue. So he chased the squirrel — and failed the test.

"How about this tree?" Luke's mom asked, pointing to a tall, fat one with lots of needles. Ranger walked all around it with Luke and Sadie.

"I like how fluffy it looks," Sadie said.

Luke pushed his face into the branches and breathed in. "I like how green it smells."

Ranger sniffed the branches. He thought it smelled good, too — fresh and sharp and winter-cool. But the needles prickled his nose. Ranger sneezed, and Luke laughed. "I think Ranger approves."

"Great!" Dad said. "We'll take it!"

They tied the tree on top of the car and drove home. Mom and Dad untied it and brought it into the living room. While they sang Christmas carols and set it in the

tree stand, Ranger went to the mudroom to get a drink of water from his dish. He was about to go find Luke when he heard a humming sound. It was coming from his dog bed.

Ranger knew that sound. He pawed at the blankets in his bed until he found the old first aid kit he'd dug up from the family's garden one day. The humming was louder now. Ranger knew what it meant. He'd heard that sound nearly a dozen times before, always when someone far away needed his help.

Once when the old metal box hummed, it had taken him to walk beside a boy named Sam on a long, dangerous journey. Once it had taken him to a stormy, flooded neighborhood where a girl needed help finding her grandmother. Once it had taken him to watch over a brother and sister who were running from people who wanted to hurt them.

Now the first aid kit was humming again.

Ranger pawed at the box's worn leather strap. He lowered his head and nuzzled it until it hung around his neck. The humming grew louder and louder. It was so loud that Ranger couldn't hear the Christmas music anymore. Light spilled from the cracks in the old box. It glowed brighter and brighter. So bright that Ranger had to close his eyes. The box grew warm at Ranger's throat. He felt like he was being squeezed through a hole in the sky.

Then suddenly, the humming stopped. Ranger opened his eyes. He was on some sort of big ship. Men in clean white uniforms walked briskly over the deck, passing one another with nods and good mornings.

Then Ranger heard another humming sound. It wasn't his first aid kit. It was a different sort of hum. It came from the sky.

And it was getting louder.

Chapter 4

BATTLE STATIONS!

Ben Hansen had just finished breakfast when he heard explosions in the distance. "What was that?"

"Probably blasting again out at Ford Island," another sailor said. "They've been doing work out there."

"On a Sunday?" Ben shook his head. Something was wrong. He hurried to the upper deck. Jerry and Chow and the other members of the USS *Arizona* Band were gathered on the deck, getting ready to play for the morning flag-raising ceremony.

On the other side of the deck, a large group of sailors stood pointing over the rail. A shaggy golden dog stood in the middle of the huddle. Everyone stared out at Ford Island. Ben ran to the rail. He couldn't believe what he was seeing.

Huge fires raged, and smoke billowed up to the sky as two airplanes flew over the island.

Airplanes! Ranger looked up just as they soared over the harbor. One swooped lower than the rest — so low that Ranger could see a man inside through the window! The crew on the deck saw him, too, and pointed.

"Army planes are out early today," one sailor said. "They're probably —"

"Army planes don't carry torpedoes!" Ben pointed as the bomber swooped low and dropped a torpedo into the water. An instant later, the *Oklahoma*, two ships ahead of them, exploded into flames.

The men on the USS *Arizona* started

running. Ranger ran alongside a tall sailor with light hair and kind, worried eyes. Ranger was worried, too. The air smelled of seawater and fire and fear. The plane that had dropped the exploding thing was circling back now, and heading straight for them.

Ranger barked.

Ben stopped running and looked down at him for a moment. "Where did you come from, dog? And what's this?" He lifted the first aid kit from Ranger's neck. But before he could open it, Ranger barked again. He pawed at Ben's leg and barked up at the sky.

Ben looked up, too. He saw the plane just an instant before it dipped low over the ship.

Then he dropped the first aid kit and shouted, "Get down!"

The sailors around him dropped to their bellies as bullets sprayed across the wooden deck. Ben's heart pounded. His breakfast felt hot in his stomach. But something made him look up.

The pilot was just overhead. Ben could see the guns aiming down at them.

"It's the Japanese!" Ben cried. He could see the big red sun on the plane's wing as it pulled up and away. Ben shouted, "Sound the air raid! The Japanese are attacking!"

Clang! Clang! Clang! went the alarm.

It was so loud it hurt Ranger's ears.

A booming voice came over the ship's speakers. "Battle stations! Battle stations! This is not a drill!"

Ben stared in a daze as men raced past him. It was really happening. They'd trained and trained for this moment, but now he felt frozen in place. The dog — where had it even come from? — nuzzled Ben's hand. He gave the dog a pat on the head.

Ranger sniffed at the young man's fingers.

He smelled like soap and pancakes and sausage. He would have liked for Ben to pet him some more, but it wasn't safe on the deck of this big ship. Not with the shooting planes flying over. Not with the terrible exploding things they dropped!

Ranger barked. He pawed at Ben until the young sailor snapped out of his daze and scrambled to his feet.

Finally, Ben's training kicked in. Everyone had to get to their battle stations. But what about the men who were still asleep? Did they even know they were under attack? Ben couldn't stop thinking about the boys still in their bunks below. He started down a ladder to check on them.

Ranger waited at the top. He didn't like ladders, but he felt a tug to stay close to this young man, so he waited while Ben climbed down and shook his fellow sailors awake.

"The Japanese are attacking!" Ben said.

They thought he was joking.

"It's real!" Ben cried. He wished he didn't have such a reputation as a prankster. Back home, April Fools' Day had always been his favorite holiday. He loved playing tricks on his mother and sisters. But this was no joke. Ben ran to the porthole. He pointed at the fires engulfing the hangars on Ford Island. "Look!"

Ranger peered down into the sleeping compartment. He wanted Ben's friends to come above deck. It wasn't safe down there! Ranger smelled smoke. Then there was a terrible bang and a rattle. The ship jolted under Ranger's paws as if something had hit it.

Ben scrambled up the ladder and nearly tripped over Ranger when he got to the top. Ben didn't have a regular battle assignment — his work was with the airplanes, and they weren't on the ship now. But he knew that every man's help would be needed. He ran for the quarterdeck.

When he got there, it was on fire! Ben hurried over to a sailor who was tugging on a fire hose. Ben pointed toward the flames. "Over here!"

"The hoses aren't working!" the other man shouted, yanking on the one he held. It was barely dripping water. It would never begin to put out the flames spreading over the deck!

Ranger's eyes and nose burned from the smoke. But he could still make out other smells on this loud, frantic ship: polished wood, hot metal, and sweat. He heard men shouting and alarms clanging, and then — a muffled cough and a wheeze, coming from an opening in the deck.

Chapter 5

RESCUE BELOW DECK

Ranger ran to the opening that led below deck. It was dark down there. He smelled smoke and hot metal and . . . a person smell!

Ranger barked. Someone was down there. Someone who needed help!

But none of the sailors on the deck were paying attention. The man below burst out coughing again.

Ranger looked down. He'd learned how to climb ladders in his search-and-rescue training with Luke and Dad. First, he'd practiced walking across a ladder that was flat on the ground. He'd learned how to place his feet, one at a time, on the rungs. Little by little, Luke and Dad raised one end of the ladder so Ranger was climbing instead of just walking.

He didn't like it at all. The wide-open spaces between the rungs made the fur on his neck feel all prickly, and he was afraid he might fall through. But Luke had placed Ranger's paws on the first rung and said, "You can do it, Ranger! You got this!" So Ranger had climbed the ladder. He went slowly at first. Sometimes he jumped off when he was partway up. But with practice, Ranger had learned to climb steeper and steeper ladders. Now he could climb the one on the slide at Luke and Sadie's favorite playground.

But this ladder wasn't going up. It was going down, and that was harder. Ranger would have to go headfirst.

Below, in the dark, the man coughed again.

Ranger stepped onto the ladder with his front paws. The metal rungs felt cold and slippery. But someone needed help, so Ranger kept going.

Front paws down a rung. Then back paws down a rung. Ranger couldn't even see where the ladder ended, but finally, he felt the floor under his paws and bounded down into the smoke.

Ranger barked, and then someone croaked out, "Here!"

Ranger found the man huddled in a corner of the small room, wheezing. Ranger nuzzled the man's hand and pawed at his arm.

The man had to get up! He had to climb out of the smoke! But he didn't move. He just kept coughing.

The tiny room was growing hotter and hotter. Ranger knew he had to get help. He nuzzled the sailor's hand once more and then went back up the ladder. The quarterdeck was packed with people, and all of them were shouting.

"Get that hose over here!"

"There's not enough water pressure!"

Ranger found Ben in the crowd of sailors. He ran to him and barked. Ben didn't look up from the fire hose, so Ranger jumped up on him.

Ben pushed him away. "Get down, dog!"

But Ranger didn't give up. He kept barking and jumping. Finally, Ben looked at him. Ranger ran to the top of the ladder and barked again. He ran back and forth until Ben followed him over.

"Anybody down there?" Ben called into the smoke. His friend Ed's bunk was down there, but Ed should have come up by now.

Ben squatted and peered into the darkness. He looked at Ranger. "You hear somebody?"

Ranger barked again, and then a muffled cough came from below.

Ben turned and climbed backward down the ladder. The sleeping compartment was so dark and smoky that he couldn't see anything.

"Where are you?" Ben called. There was no answer. Or if there was, the chaos coming from above deck drowned it out. "Help me out, mate! We need to get you out of here!"

Ben felt along the wall as he headed for the far corner of the bunk. After a few steps, his foot hit something soft and he heard a quiet "Oof!"

He bent down and felt around until he touched the man's shoulder. "Ed, is that you? Are you all right?" Ben asked. Ed gasped but couldn't answer. Ben grabbed his arm and tried to help him stand, but he was too weak.

Now Ben was coughing, too. The small space was too hot and smoky. If he stayed there much longer, he'd pass out. He grabbed hold of Ed's leg and dragged him to the ladder.

"Come on now!" Ben tried to push his friend up the rungs. "Up you go! If you stay, you're going to die down here!"

But Ed was too weak to climb. And he was too heavy to lift. Finally, Ben looked up and saw Ranger.

"Get help!" he shouted up at the dog. "Go find help!"

Find? Ranger barked.

Find!

Ranger understood that Ben needed help. He raced over to the men who were struggling with the broken fire hose. Ranger barked and barked, but they couldn't hear him over the ship's alarms and panicked shouting. The fire was spreading. The smoke was thicker and the voices louder.

Ranger jumped up on a short sailor and

pawed at his chest. The man spun around and shoved him down. But Ranger jumped up again. Then he raced back and forth between the ladder and the sailor, pawing and barking, until the man's eyes opened wide. He grabbed another sailor by the arm. "Someone's down there!" he shouted, and pointed.

Ranger waited on the upper deck while the two men climbed down into the dark to join Ben. Ben grabbed Ed by the belt and worked with the other sailors to haul him up the ladder into the fresh air.

"He needs medical attention!" Ben said. "We have to —"

BOOM!

Ben hit the deck and covered his head. A wave of heat washed over him. When it passed, he looked up. A bomb had hit the turret and blasted through the quarterdeck. Now the

deck below was on fire, too. Flames shot up from the hole like a torch.

"Man the fire hose!" someone shouted. Another sailor dragged a hose over, but the water pressure wasn't strong enough. The fire kept spreading.

"Take cover!" another sailor shouted.

Ben looked up to see a new group of planes approaching. They were heading straight for Battleship Row.

Chapter 6

ATTACK ON BATTLESHIP ROW

"Grace!" Paul Yamada shouted his sister's name over the roar of planes and gunfire. He crouched low in their little rowboat. "Get down!"

Grace ducked and covered her head as bullets sprayed over the waves. "We have to get to the island!" she cried.

Paul shook his head. "They're attacking it!" He pulled hard on one oar to turn. "We have to head back!"

It had been only minutes since they'd spotted the first Japanese planes flying in over the mountains. Now bombers filled the sky, flying in formation. The air was thick with smoke. Paul's heart pounded. He pulled harder on the oars. But where should they even go? The entire harbor was full of smoke and flames.

A new group of planes turned. Paul gripped the oars, frozen in place as the planes swooped lower. They were coming in fast.

"Those bombers are after the battleships!" Grace cried as the first plane dropped its torpedo. Paul had read enough war comics to know how torpedoes worked. When planes dropped them, the torpedoes became underwater missiles. He watched the first one disappear into the waves and held his breath as it barreled toward its target.

Seconds later, the ship exploded in a burst of flames and black smoke. Paul could feel the heat on his face. Then another blast echoed over the harbor. And another! Booms shook the sky.

Another plane buzzed low over them. Any second, one of the bombs would find their little boat. There was no escape. There was nowhere to hide.

Paul dropped the oars. He put his hands over his ears and squeezed his eyes shut to block it all out.

"Paul!" Grace shouted. "Paul! We have to get out of here!" She lurched across the boat and stumbled toward him, grabbing for the oars.

It shook Paul out of his terrified daze. He took the oars from her and started rowing again. "I'm sorry, I just —" He swallowed hard. He couldn't admit to his sister that for all of his Captain America talk, he was terrified. He could barely breathe as bombs exploded around them and even more planes buzzed overhead. He didn't know what Captain America would do now, but all he could do was row. So he tugged on the oars, inching them back toward the dock they'd set off from less than an hour ago. Away from the battleships. Away from the worst of the attack.

Paul's heart pounded with the effort. His throat burned from the smoke, and his eyes stung with tears. But as he rowed toward shore, he couldn't stop staring past Grace, out at the battleships. All around them, debris floated in the water.

Paul could still hear the blasts and the diving planes. He heard the *rat-a-tat-a-tat* of machine guns as ships fired back at the attacking planes. And now there was another sound, too. A quieter, haunting sound amid all the chaos. The cries of injured sailors drifted over the waves.

"Grace, look!" There were men in the water. Dozens of them.

Grace looked back, and Paul heard her gasp. Then she turned to face him. "We can't leave now!" she said.

Paul swallowed hard. He held the oars loose in his hands and felt the waves tugging at them. His sister's words tugged at the rest of him.

Grace had a huge heart. When she grew up, she wanted to be a nurse, just like Helen. But did she really understand what it meant to put themselves in the line of fire? The Japanese planes weren't letting up. If anything, more were streaming into the harbor. Their little rowboat would be an easy target for low-flying gunners.

Still, Paul couldn't stop thinking about the heroes in Jimmy's comics. They never ran from

danger. They never left someone to face trouble alone.

Grace shouted what he already knew. "We have to help them!"

She was right. They had to go back. Paul took a deep breath. He pulled hard on the right oar.

Just as the rowboat started to turn, a bomb fell from a plane high above. It landed on one of the giant battleships, and the whole harbor lit up in flames.

Chapter 7

SURVIVAL IN A FIERY SEA

Ranger was staring up at the planes when the bomb hit.

First, there was a jolt. The big ship shuddered under his paws. Then a massive explosion shook the sky. The blast raised the battleship right out of the water. It jumped up from the sea and splashed down again, as if it were trying to shake off its crew.

Ben dropped the hose he'd been holding and covered his head as a fireball roared toward them. Ranger crouched low beside him and closed his eyes. A terrible wave of heat and smoke and noise blasted him from the deck. *WHOOSH!* It was as if an enormous, flaming giant had knocked him clear off the ship.

The next thing Ranger knew, he was in the water. It was cold and pressing on him all around. He paddled and kicked and fought his way to the surface until finally his face burst up from the waves.

Ranger sucked in a breath and barked. The air was full of smoke and screams. It smelled sharp and dangerous — like fire and oil and hot, hot steel. Above him, what was left of the ship was engulfed in flames. Even the ocean was on fire! Smoke and flames licked up from patches of oil on the surface.

Ranger paddled through the waves, trying to keep his face out of the water. The sea was coated in oil that stung Ranger's eyes and made it almost impossible to swim. No matter how hard he paddled, he couldn't push it away.

And where was Ben? The young sailor had been right next to Ranger on the deck.

Ranger turned to look back at the ship. He couldn't see anyone alive in the smoke and ruin. The ship's decks were engulfed in flames, and it was already sinking. Ben must have been blasted into the water, too.

Ranger swam as best he could through the hot oil. He ignored the whirring plane engines and explosions all around him. He tried to keep his head above water so he could sniff the air.

Mostly, he smelled smoke. But there were other scents floating over the waves, too — ocean water and oil and fear. Another plane swooped low above him, buzzing and blasting the sea with gunfire. Water sprayed up around him and splashed in his face.

Ranger struggled to keep his nose above the waves. He sniffed the salty air until finally . . . there!

It was faint, mixed with the smells of smoke and seawater, but it was definitely the Ben person! Ranger kept paddling until he spotted Ben's light hair above the waves. Ben was trying to swim through the oily water, too. He was having even more trouble than Ranger. Every so often, his head would slip below the surface. Then he'd burst up again, sputtering and coughing.

Ranger wanted to paddle faster, but the oil slowed him down. When he finally got close to Ben, the young man was flailing in the water, barely afloat. Ranger barked at him.

"Dog!" Ben called out, and then swallowed a mouthful of water. He gasped and coughed and reached out to Ranger, splashing at the oily waves. No matter how hard he tried to swim, the oil seemed to keep him from moving. His whole left side had been badly burned when the fireball from the explosion blasted him off the ship. The salt water stung his wounds. Every time he moved, pain shot down his side.

More than anything, Ben was thinking about his friends. They'd been standing beside him on the deck of the ship. Where were they all now? Had they been thrown into the water like him and the dog? When he looked back at the *Arizona*, sinking and in flames, he hoped so. That was their only chance.

But how much hope was there, really? When Ben had first surfaced after the blast, he'd started swimming toward Ford Island. Soon it became clear that he'd never make it. He was badly burned and already exhausted. Instead, he'd turned toward the *Nevada*, but now it was on fire, too. He was trying to stay calm, to rely on his training, but with every second that passed, it was harder to keep his head above water. Each time he slipped beneath the waves, he thought about giving up.

He tried to stay strong by remembering his family back home. He thought about his sisters and his mother. Ben reached down to feel his pocket. His poem was still there, through the blasts and the fire and the sea.

Little Boy kneels at the foot of the bed . . .

Ben's head slipped below the waves and he inhaled a mouthful of water. He pushed himself back up and coughed it out.

Droops on the little hands little gold head.
Hush! Hush! Whisper who dares . . .

He couldn't give up. Not yet. But he was so tired.

Ranger barked again, and Ben looked at him. "Get help, dog!" He choked out the words, gasping. "Find help!"

Find? Ranger wanted to help Ben *now*. But he knew he couldn't get closer or Ben would pull him under the water. Ben needed *real* help!

Ranger barked once more. Then he turned and started swimming away. He lifted his head high above the waves, searching for someone — anyone — who could help Ben. There were other men in the water, but they were all hurt and scared and exhausted, too. Some of them weren't moving at all.

So Ranger kept paddling. Finally, he saw a small boat up ahead with people in it. The people weren't very big. They looked more like kids than rescuers, but maybe they would be able to help. Ranger knew Ben couldn't stay afloat much longer.

Ranger couldn't swim much longer, either.

He didn't know if he could make it all the way to the little boat in this awful fiery water with the planes buzzing all around. But he knew he had to try.

Chapter 8

RESCUE FROM THE WAVES

"What's that?" Grace pointed past Paul's shoulder.

He didn't want to look. He felt braver rowing toward the smoke and fire when he didn't have to stare into the chaos. But Grace kept pointing, so Paul twisted around. "Is that . . ." He squinted into the smoke. Then he heard barking. "It's a dog!" Paul started rowing again.

Ranger barked some more. When he was sure the kids in the boat had seen him, he turned and started swimming back toward Ben. They had to come. They had to help Ben!

Every once in a while, Ranger would pause and bark again.

"He keeps swimming away!" Grace said as Paul rowed. Another explosion roared through the harbor, and she shuddered. "Maybe . . . maybe we should go back."

Paul glanced over his shoulder just as the dog barked again. He kept doing that, barking and then swimming away. Paul looked past the dog's bobbing head and saw something else in the water. "He's found someone!"

Paul pulled harder on the oars. Blisters on his hands had torn open, and his palms felt as if they were on fire. Soon, the rowboat was close enough for Paul to see the face of a young man struggling in the water. He wasn't swimming. Not really. Just splashing up and down, trying not to drown.

"Here!" Paul tossed the man the life preserver that his father insisted they keep on the boat.

Ben didn't see it. He didn't hear Paul call to him. His eyes burned with smoke. His ears still rang from the explosion on the *Arizona*, and his mouth was full of seawater. He couldn't hold on anymore.

Ranger swam to the floating ring in the water. He nudged it toward Ben with his nose. But the sailor just flailed at it and pushed it away.

Ranger barked. He pushed the life preserver at Ben's face, barking again and again. Finally, Ben's hand came down on it. He pulled it to his chest and clung to it, gasping for breath.

"You're going to be all right!" Grace called from the rowboat. She started to reach out to Ben, but Paul pulled her back.

"Wait!" Paul whispered. "We can't get him into the boat until he settles down. He could capsize us, and then we'll all be in trouble."

Grace nodded. She turned back to the

sailor in the water. "You're going to be all right," she said again, quietly this time. "I'm Grace Yamada. What's your name?"

"Ben." The sailor's voice was raspy and weak.

"Hey, Ben. I'm Paul. Take some breaths and try to relax, okay?" Paul said. "Then we'll be able to get you into the boat."

Ben nodded and took a shaky breath. Ranger swam closer to him and nuzzled his shoulder.

"Your dog sure was looking out for you," Grace said. "He came to get us, and now we can take you to shore. Our sister is a nurse, and she'll be able to help."

"Ready to come in the boat?" Paul asked. The man nodded, so Paul rowed closer. "Grab on to the side and then reach for us. Easy now . . ." Paul and Grace each took one of Ben's hands. They shifted their weight to the other side of the boat so it wouldn't tip. Then they held on as Ben pulled himself up, groaning. He flung a leg over the rail of the boat and flopped inside. Grace gave him a drink of water, and Paul wrapped a jacket around his shoulders.

"Look!" Grace pointed to something floating in the water.

Paul used the oar to pull it closer, then reached down to fish it out of the waves. "It's a first aid kit." He opened it, and water spilled out.

Ranger barked.

"Keep that," Grace told Paul. "The bandages are ruined but maybe there's ointment or something we can use to help him." She nodded toward Ben. Then she turned to Ranger. "You're next, dog. Come on!" She patted the side of the boat with her hand.

Ranger swam toward the boat just as another plane buzzed overhead.

Paul looked up. "Grace, we really need to —"

"We can't leave him!" Grace said, and thumped the boat again. "Here, boy!"

Ranger paddled up, and Grace reached down to grab him under his front legs. "Come on now!" She leaned away and hauled him into the boat so fast that they both tumbled backward.

Ranger climbed off Grace and shook himself. Then he carefully climbed over the bench to Ben. The young sailor was shivering uncontrollably in the bottom of the boat.

Another explosion boomed out over the harbor as Paul picked up the oars and started to row.

Ranger stayed close to Ben as the boat slipped through the smoke. Ben was out of the water, but he wasn't out of danger. None of them were.

Chapter 9

DANGEROUS BOOKS

Ranger sat with Grace in the back of the boat while Paul rowed. Fires still raged on the battleships. Most of Ben's ship had already disappeared beneath the rippling waves. The others looked like ghosts in the thick black smoke. But at least the buzzing planes had finally faded away.

Ranger's first aid kit was tucked under the front bench of the rowboat, dripping and quiet. Ranger had found help for Ben, but he understood that it wasn't time to go home. Not yet. He had more work to do.

After a slow, sloshy ride, the rowboat bumped up against the rocks on shore. Paul and Grace climbed out and held their hands out to Ben. He'd been curled up in the bow of the little rowboat, shivering. Now he pressed against the bench and tried to stand. The boat wobbled under his feet, and he would have fallen if Paul hadn't grabbed his arm to steady him.

Ben's shoes and clothes were coated in oil from the filthy water. He slipped on the rocks when Paul and Grace finally helped him out of the boat and onto shore. With every movement, his wet clothes brushed against his burns, and pain pulsed through his body. He didn't know where they were going now, but he knew he couldn't make it far. "I don't think I can walk much more," he said.

"It's all right." Paul hurried to a clearing in the brush nearby and wheeled out a small cart. "We normally use this to carry eggs and vegetables — not people," he explained. "It may not be very comfortable, but you won't have to walk the mile to our house."

Ben leaned against the cart, hesitating. He could tell that Paul and Grace were of Japanese descent. Even before the morning attack, there had been whispers on the ship about spies. Paul and Grace were just kids, but what about their parents? And what would happen to him if he were found in a home owned by a Japanese family?

"Wait . . ." Grace went back to the boat and grabbed a jacket and the first aid kit. She tucked the kit into a corner of the cart and folded the jacket over it as a sort of pillow. "It'll help a little, at least." She held out her hand.

Ben's eyes burned. Not from the smoke now, but from her kindness. All she wanted was to help him. Ben lowered himself into the cart and tucked his long legs inside. He couldn't think right now about what the attack would mean for families like Paul and Grace's. He needed medical attention. He had to find Jerry and Chow and his other fellow sailors. But first, he had to survive the long, bumpy ride to the Yamadas' house. Every rut in the road made him cry out with pain.

"Sorry!" Paul called. He was doing his best, but Ben was heavy, and the road was a mess. When he'd been out in the rowboat, Paul had figured the Japanese planes were only attacking the military base. But there was also smoke coming from the neighborhood up ahead — *his* neighborhood.

"Stay with him while I find Helen," Paul told Grace when they finally reached their family's home. He ran inside, but his sister and father were gone. His mother was gathering up books in her arms and arguing with his grandmother.

"Mama, where are Papa and Helen?" Paul asked.

"They've gone out to offer help," she said, snatching another book from the shelf.

"What are you doing?" Paul asked.

"She is burning our history," Obaachan said. Tears streamed down her face.

Paul stared at the stack in his mother's arms. They were all of the family's Japanese books. He looked at the bare living room wall, where there used to be a fancy Japanese scroll — a gift from the governor of the district where his grandfather once lived in Japan.

His mother saw him staring. "I burned it," she whispered. "And these must go, too!" She nodded down at the books. "Anything the

Americans find here could be dangerous for us."

Paul's head was spinning. The Yamadas *were* Americans! Ojiichan and Obaachan had been born in Japan. But Paul's parents and all of his siblings had been born here in Hawaii. How could his mother think the government would blame them for the Japanese attack? For the explosions and the fires on the ships?

The whole morning at the harbor flashed through Paul's mind. When it did, he remembered Ben in the cart outside. He put a hand on his mother's arm. "Mama," he said. "Grace and I have brought a sailor who needs help. He's hurt."

His mother's eyes grew wide. She dropped the books and followed him outside. When she saw Ben in the cart, she sucked in her breath. He was barely conscious, and his breathing was shallow. The shaggy, wet dog sat by the cart, nuzzling the sailor's arm and licking his hand.

"He needs to get to a hospital." Mrs. Yamada glanced back at the house. Then she looked at Paul and Grace. "Helen and Papa are already on the way there to help. Take this man to them. And then come straight home. Do you hear me?" Her eyes shined with tears. "For our family, I fear the worst of this is yet to come."

Chapter 10

ANOTHER ATTACK

It wasn't even nine o'clock yet when Paul and Grace set out for the hospital. They each took a handle of the cart and pushed it up the bumpy street.

Ranger trotted along beside them. His fur was wet and matted with oil. He wanted to go home. But his first aid kit was tucked alongside Ben in the cart. Still quiet. His work here wasn't done. They had to get Ben to someone who could care for him.

Ranger was also worried about Paul and Grace. Even though the buzzing planes were gone, few people were in the streets. The warm wind crackled with danger. It smelled of hot metal, seawater, and smoke. Radio news reports drifted out living room windows. "Stay in your homes," the announcers said. "Keep your radios on."

Paul walked past the grocery store, the soda fountain, and the barbershop in a daze. He was almost to his friend Jimmy's house when he heard a sound that made him stop walking.

Ranger heard it, too. A high buzzing that came from above. It made the fur on his neck prickle. Ranger barked. He pawed at Paul's leg.

"Easy, dog," Paul said, searching the sky. He looked at Grace. "Do you hear that?"

She nodded. Then the planes soared into view. The attack wasn't over.

Another fleet of Japanese bombers swooped in over the city, heading for the harbor. Paul looked around, but there was no place to take cover.

"Get low!" Paul shouted to Grace, and they both crouched down next to the cart.

Ranger huddled beside them. He could feel Paul's heart thumping through the boy's thin shirt as the planes buzzed overhead.

Boom!

An explosion shook the street. It was close. Too close!

Ranger barked, but there was nothing he could do to stop the planes, and nothing he could do to keep the bombs from falling.

Boom!

Rat-a-tat-a-tat!

This time, the Americans must have been ready. Antiaircraft fire exploded in the sky. Paul covered his head with his hands.

Ben stirred in the cart. He was so hurt, so

weak, and barely awake. Now the very air seemed to be exploding around him. This wasn't the USS *Arizona*. Where was he? And why was the sky on fire?

All at once, Ben remembered the planes and the explosions. He remembered his struggle to get the hoses working, the fireball that blasted him off the ship, the sea that wanted to swallow him up, and his fight to the surface. He remembered swimming and swimming through the fiery, oil-covered waves until he couldn't keep his head above water anymore. He remembered reaching for his pocket . . . his mother's poem . . .

Little Boy kneels at the foot of the bed . . .

He remembered fighting to stay afloat, swimming . . . swimming . . .

And then . . . had there been a dog?

Ben turned his head and saw Ranger

huddled by the cart with Paul and Grace. He put his hand out over the edge of the cart. Soon, he felt a wet nose nuzzling it.

Ranger licked Ben's fingers. When Ben moved his hand onto Ranger's head, Ranger leaned into it. Sometimes at home, Luke would keep his hand on Ranger's head that way, too, when Luke was feeling scared or sad. When that happened, Ranger always stayed right there beside him. He did that for Ben, too, even as the planes roared overhead. There was nothing he could do to stop them. But he could be there for Ben.

Finally, the planes tipped their wings and flew away. Paul's heart pounded and his black hair dripped with sweat. His hands clenched the cart handle so hard that the grain of the wood was imprinted on his palms. He looked at Grace, who was still staring into the sky, eyes wide. "We're okay," he said. "Come on . . . let's go."

"But the hospital is so far!" Grace's voice trembled. "What if the planes come back?"

Paul looked at the sky. The planes were gone. For now. But that didn't mean the battle was over. "We're close to Jimmy Abe's house," he said. It was just around the corner, and his mother was a nurse. "Maybe Mrs. Abe can help." Paul wanted to believe she would. He wanted to believe they'd all be safe. He took a shaky breath. They had to keep going. They had to make sure Ben was all right. They'd promised him that when they hauled him out of the oily sea. They had to get him help. It was only one more block . . .

But when Paul turned the corner, he felt as if someone had punched him in the stomach. Jimmy Abe's house was engulfed in flames.

"No!" Paul dropped the cart handle and ran to the front porch. Black smoke poured from the open door. It filled his nose and mouth. "Jimmy!" He choked out the name and waited. But there was no answer. "Mrs. Abe! Mr. Abe!"

Ranger ran onto the porch beside Paul. The boy was too close to the burning building. It wasn't safe! Ranger barked and pawed at Paul's leg.

"Get down, dog!" Paul pushed him away and banged on a window. "Jimmy!" he shouted again, peering through the glass. All he could see was smoke and darkness. But then a muffled, choked voice cried out from inside.

"Help!"

Chapter 11

DARKNESS AND SMOKE

"Jimmy!" Paul shouted into the darkness. He took a step inside and tried to call out again, but the awful smoke filled his mouth and his nose. He stumbled backward, coughing.

Ranger ran to Paul and nuzzled his hand. Paul sank to his knees and wrapped his arms around the wet dog's neck. "My friend is in there." His voice broke, and tears streamed down his face. "Someone has to find him!"

Find? Ranger barked.

Paul stood up and swiped at his tears with the back of his hand. He stared down at

Ranger. "Can you find him?" He pointed into the house. "Find Jimmy!"

Find!

Ranger was good at finding people. During his search-and-rescue training, he'd practiced finding Luke in all kinds of places. He'd found Luke in thick woods and in wintry fields, buried in the snow. He'd found him hiding in barrels and tucked into corners of old, run-down buildings. But this building was more than run-down. It was smoky and unstable, and its roof was on fire.

Ranger stepped toward the door. He could hear someone coughing inside. He could smell burning wood, charred furniture, and hot, hot metal. But he could smell something else, too — a person smell. Maybe it was the Jimmy person Paul was calling.

Ranger crouched low to the floor, where the smoke wasn't so thick, and crept into the house. The entry was dark and smoky. There were stairs going up, but a beam had fallen across them. That's not where the smell was, anyway.

Ranger sniffed the air close to the wood floor. It smelled like ash and dust and shoes, but there was a person smell, too. Ranger followed that scent down a hallway to the kitchen, where part of the roof had collapsed onto the table. The fire smell was stronger here. Smoke burned Ranger's eyes and stung his nose, but he kept searching. When he crept closer to the table, the person smell got stronger.

There!

A boy around Luke and Paul's age was crouched under the table, wheezing and holding his knee.

Ranger barked and ran up to the boy. He had to get out of there! Some of the roof shingles that had fallen into the kitchen were on

fire. Now the flames were licking at the cabinets.

The boy coughed, but he didn't come out from under the table. Ranger crouched low and crawled next to him. Ranger nuzzled the boy's cheek, and the boy reached out to pat his head.

Ranger stepped back and barked. He loved pats and ear scratches, but there was no time for that now. The boy had to get out! Ranger barked again. He went back and pawed at the boy's leg.

The boy winced, and then Ranger understood. He was hurt. The bottom part of his leg was trapped under some sort of beam that had fallen. Every time the boy tried to move it, he cried out in pain and then coughed again.

The smoke was getting thicker. Once the fire from the shingles reached the curtains, the whole kitchen would go up in flames! The boy couldn't stay here. But Ranger couldn't get him out.

Ranger nuzzled the boy's hand and hoped he would understand that Ranger wasn't leaving him. Not for long, anyway.

Ranger had to go get help. That's what he had learned in search-and-rescue training with Dad and Luke. Usually, when Ranger found a person, it was his job to stay with the person and bark until someone came to help. But sometimes that wasn't enough.

Chapter 12

ARE YOU AN AMERICAN?

Ranger crouched low and climbed out from under the table. He made his way through the smoke to the door and bounded down the porch steps. Paul and Grace were still there with Ben, but neither was big enough to move the beam and help the boy inside. Ranger looked up and down the street until he spotted a man walking toward them from down the block. He raced up to him, barking, and jumped on him.

"Down!" The man swatted at Ranger. He had black hair like Paul and Grace's. Ranger barked and jumped up on him again. Then Ranger ran toward Paul and Grace and the house with the trapped boy. He ran back to the man and barked again. The man stared up ahead. Then he started running, too.

"Papa!" Paul cried out, and ran into his father's arms. But right away he pulled back and blurted out all that had happened — the rowboat and the planes and the bombs, the injured sailor and the dog and now this. Paul pointed to the house. "Jimmy is in there! I heard him, and the dog went in, but . . ."

Ranger barked and pawed at Mr. Yamada's leg. Then Ranger climbed onto the porch. Mr. Yamada stepped up, too. When Ranger went inside, Mr. Yamada followed him. He dropped to his hands and knees and crawled down the hallway.

The smoke was even thicker now. Ranger couldn't hear the Jimmy boy anymore. But when they reached the kitchen, Ranger crouched under the table and barked.

"Hold on, son!" Mr. Yamada moved the table. He crouched low and lifted the heavy beam from Jimmy's leg. "You have to move!" he grunted, straining under the weight of the beam.

Ranger barked at Jimmy, but the boy seemed frozen in place. The flames from the shingles were licking at the kitchen curtains now. They had to get out! Mr. Yamada couldn't hold up the beam for long.

Ranger barked again. He licked the boy's face and pawed at his chest until Jimmy leaned forward onto his arms and dragged himself out from under the beam. Mr. Yamada dropped it, rushed to Jimmy's side, and pulled him up to stand. "Come on, now," he said, and helped the boy through the smoky hallway and outside.

"Jimmy!" Paul ran to his father's side and took his friend's other arm.

"Is anyone else inside?" Mr. Yamada asked.

Jimmy shook his head. "My mother went to the hospital to help, and my father . . ." He hesitated. "The soldiers came to our house and took him away."

"What?" Paul stared at his friend. "Why?" Mr. Abe taught Japanese language and culture in classes Paul and Grace took after school. But Mr. Abe was an American. He'd been born in Hawaii, just like Paul's family. "How can they do that?"

"They said he shouldn't be teaching Japanese language in America." Jimmy swallowed hard. "They took him . . . I don't know where. Somewhere to answer more questions."

"Don't worry," Mr. Yamada said. "He'll be all right. This is America. There are laws to protect citizens. For now, we should get your leg looked at, so —"

"What is your name?" someone shouted. Three soldiers in uniform stood in the street. One of them pointed at Paul's father. "You! What is your name?"

Paul's father held his hands in front of him and slowly walked down the porch steps to the street. "My name is Iku Yamada."

"What are you doing?"

"Helping my son's friend. He needs to see a doctor." Mr. Yamada pointed to Jimmy, but the soldiers kept asking questions.

"Are you a citizen of the United States?" a soldier asked.

"Yes, I was born here on Oahu," Mr. Yamada said.

The soldiers looked at one another. "You will have to come with us." They took his arm and started to lead him away.

"Papa!" Paul cried out. His heart filled with rage. How could this be happening? After everything they'd been through already this morning? "He's done nothing wrong! Why are you taking him away?"

The soldiers didn't answer.

"Take Jimmy to the hospital and find Helen!" Mr. Yamada called. "And then go straight home. I'll be there as soon as I can." He tried to smile, but Paul heard the fear in his voice as the soldiers led him away.

Paul wanted to chase after them. He wanted to cling to his father and never let go. But he had to be strong. A Captain America kind of strong. For his father, and for Jimmy and Ben.

"Can you walk?" Paul asked Jimmy, who was leaning against a neighbor's truck, still coughing.

"I think so." He took a few limping steps. "But I don't want to leave."

"You have to see a doctor," Grace said.

"I know." Jimmy coughed again and looked up at the smoke pouring from what was left of his family's house. "What if my father comes back?"

"He'll wait for you," Paul promised. He could see the worry in his friend's eyes. He felt it, too. And he felt the quiet weight of the question Jimmy hadn't asked. What if their fathers didn't come back at all?

Chapter 13

TOO MANY TO HELP

Paul and Grace lifted the cart handles and started out. Jimmy limped along, holding the edge of the cart to steady himself. Every block felt like a mile. The whole sky was black with smoke, as if the sun might never shine again.

And the planes were still coming. Every time a new formation buzzed overhead, Paul's heart jumped into his throat and he held his breath. Every time they passed over, he let it out.

Even though he couldn't see the bombs falling, he couldn't help thinking about where they might be landing. Paul didn't know where his father was being taken, but he said a quiet prayer for his safety, and for the rest of their family. Would the Japanese target the hospital where Helen was working? Would his mother and grandmother be safe at home?

"Hold on." After the planes had gone, Grace dropped the cart. She'd been checking on Ben every so often and making him drink a little water. This time, she couldn't get him to take any. She shook her head, and they continued down the street.

Jimmy's house wasn't the only one that had been damaged. Paul and Grace wheeled the cart past three more that had been hit. Smoking debris littered the empty streets. Paul couldn't believe this was the same neighborhood that had been so lively and friendly just the day before, with everyone starting to get ready for the holidays. Paul's family always walked from house to house on New Year's Day to celebrate. In the days leading up to the holiday, all the neighbors would gather together to make mochi, steaming the sweet rice and pounding it into treats for the celebration. It was supposed to be a joyful time of beginnings. Now everyone was talking about war. Would they even celebrate this year? It felt as if the clouds of black smoke had swallowed up all of his family's traditions.

But Paul couldn't think about that. They had to get Ben and Jimmy to the hospital. Helen would be there. She would be safe, and she would help. Then they would go home, and Papa would be waiting with Mama and Obaachan. They would all be safe, and they would be together, and then . . . well, then they could face whatever was coming.

Finally, they reached the hospital. The whole block swarmed with people. Some ran crying through the streets. Some pushed wounded people in carts like the one that held Ben. Some held up their loved ones, calling out for help. Doctors and nurses hurried everywhere, trying to bring in the patients who needed help the most. But Helen was nowhere to be found.

"Should we just go in?" Grace suddenly sounded nervous. Paul understood. After the way the soldiers had treated his father, Paul was afraid to ask anyone for help. But he nodded. They'd come all this way, and Ben seemed to be slipping away. His breathing was shallow and fast, and the color had drained from his face.

"Excuse me!" Paul said, pushing the cart forward. "We have an injured sailor who needs help!" He waved and kept shouting until a hospital worker came over. The man took one look at Ben and waved to two other men for help. They lifted Ben from the cart, loaded him onto a stretcher, and hurried him inside. Paul and Grace didn't even get to say good-bye.

A kind-looking nurse stepped up to them. "Are you hurt?" she asked. "Or looking for someone?"

"My friend's leg is hurt," Paul said, and pointed to Jimmy, who was slumped on the steps. Another nurse was already talking to him, rolling up his pant leg to look at his injury. Paul looked more closely. "That's Jimmy's mother!" He looked up at the first nurse. "He's all right, miss. And so are we. But thank you."

"We need to find our sister," Grace said. "Helen Yamada."

"I can help you with that," the nurse said, and led them inside.

Find? Ranger's ears perked up, and he followed them into the hospital.

Paul thought about telling the dog no — it was a hospital, after all — but he'd been with them all this time. Without the dog, they never would have found Ben. Without the dog, Jimmy might never have made it out of his house. And the hospital was so busy that no one seemed to notice, anyway.

The nurse led them down a hallway and stopped beside a door. "Wait here," she said, and stepped inside.

Paul and Grace stood with Ranger in the crowded hall. It was filled with patients on stretchers and wheelchairs. Some of them wore uniforms like Ben's. But none of the uniforms were white anymore. They were wet and black with oil, or worse, stained with blood.

Paul still couldn't believe everything that had happened. And now they'd probably be at war. War! Would there be more attacks? Would people blame his family and other Japanese Americans for the bombings? It made him sick to think about, so he reached down and gave the wet dog a pat on the head.

Ranger leaned into Paul's hand. He'd left his first aid kit in the cart outside. He couldn't go home. Not yet. Paul and Grace were alone and afraid, and they needed him. Paul kept patting Ranger's head. Grace slumped down the wall, sat beside him, and wrapped her arms around his neck. They stayed that way for a long time until the nurse came back.

"I think your sister is in this unit," the nurse said, opening the door.

"There she is!" Paul's heart flooded with relief.

Helen stood in the middle of a busy room crowded with patients. Her hands held a pile of bandages and her face was full of concern.

When she looked up, her mouth dropped open. "Paul! Grace!" She ran to them and pulled them into a hug. "Where have you been? Why are you out? What are you doing here? Are you all right?"

"We're fine," Paul said. Helen held her siblings back from her for a moment and looked them over. When she was satisfied that Paul was telling the truth, she pulled them into her arms again and took a deep breath. "It's been awful here. There are so many sailors wounded, and so many who didn't make it. We're trying to help as many as we can."

"We helped a sailor, too!" Grace said. "We found him in the harbor and brought him here and — that's him!" She pointed past Helen. A nurse was wheeling Ben across the room in a wheelchair. Just as Grace started toward him, two soldiers appeared in the door of the room.

"Helen Yamada?" one of them boomed.

Paul's stomach lurched into his throat. *No, no, no*, he thought. They couldn't take Helen away, too. She was helping people! And she was all he and Grace had right now.

"Yes?" Helen stepped forward. "That's me."

One of the soldiers took her by the arm. "Please come with me."

Chapter 14

HUSH! HUSH!

No! Paul thought again as the soldier led Helen into the hallway. But then he heard her cry out with joy.

"Papa!"

Paul ran to the door. His father was there, holding on to Helen's hands. When he saw Paul and Grace, he wrapped them up in his arms. "Thank goodness you made it," he said. "Thank goodness my children are all right."

"What happened?" Paul asked him.

"They took me to the police station for

more questions," Papa said. "Then they told me I was free to go."

"Did they let Mr. Abe go, too?" Grace asked.

His smile faded. "Not yet, I'm afraid."

"Have you been home?" Paul asked. "Are Mama and Obaachan all right?"

Their father nodded. "They are safe at home. And we need to get you there, too. Is Jimmy being treated?"

Grace nodded. "His mother was here, and she's with him. He's all right. And the sailor we helped is here, too!"

Paul was glad they'd found Ben. Now at least they'd have a chance to say good-bye before they left. "Can we go back and see him? Please?"

His father nodded, so they went back into the patient room and found Ben in a wheel-chair by the far wall. His face had been cleaned up a little, and he had a tube in his arm, giving him fluids. He already looked better. More alert. He saw Paul and Grace and motioned them over.

Ben searched their faces. "I'm sorry," he said. "I can't remember your names."

"Grace," she said. "And my brother is Paul."

"Grace. And Paul." Ben took a shaky breath and looked at them. "Thank you." His voice broke, and he looked down at his hands. Paul saw that he was clutching a tattered card with writing on it. "If you hadn't found me, there's no way I would be alive now."

"It was the dog," Paul said, and patted the side of his leg. Ranger trotted over and licked Ben's hand.

Ben stared at him. All that time he'd been drifting in and out of consciousness, he'd wondered if he had imagined it. But no, the shaggy golden dog was real. Here in the hospital. And now he remembered everything. How the dog had appeared on the ship just before the explosion. How it had paddled by his side in the water. How it wouldn't let him give up. The dog had left him then, but now he understood that it had only gone to find help. The dog had found Paul and Grace, who brought Ben here.

And now . . . now he was safe. He was going to be all right. He was hurt, but he would heal. He would get to go home. He'd get to see his mother again.

Hush! Hush! Whisper who dares . . .

He'd tell her how her poem had kept him from giving up.

Ben leaned forward. He held Ranger's head in his hands and brought his face close. "Thank you, dog," he whispered. Tears streamed down his face. "Thank you."

"Who let the dog in here?" a doctor boomed. "This is a hospital, not an animal shelter!"

"We'll take him out," Paul's father said. He

looked down at Ben. "We have to go now. But thank you for your service and your sacrifice today."

"Thank you for yours," Ben said. He shook Paul's and Grace's hands, and they went to say good-bye to Helen, who was staying at the hospital to work an extra shift.

Ranger started to walk away, but Ben said, "Wait, dog," and patted his knee.

Ranger came back.

"Here . . . I want you to have this." Ben tucked the worn paper he'd been holding under Ranger's collar. "It's something my mother gave me, to keep until I came home safe." His eyes filled with tears. "I'm going home now, thanks to you, so I don't need it anymore. You keep it, and remember me, all right?"

"Get the dog out of here!" the doctor shouted again.

Ranger nuzzled Ben's hand one last time.

Then he followed Paul and Grace and their father out of the room, down the hall, and outside.

"We left the cart here somewhere." Paul found it, tipped over at the side of the hospital steps. He righted it and pushed it down the sidewalk to where his father and Grace were waiting.

"You coming, dog?" Paul said. He didn't know if Captain America had a pet, but he was pretty sure that his parents would let this shaggy dog stay with them, at least for a while, after all he'd done to help today. "You can come home with us, you know."

Ranger trotted over to Paul and let him scratch his ear. Paul was a very good ear scratcher. But Ranger wasn't coming. A humming sound caught his attention. It was coming from the grass where the cart had been.

Ranger nuzzled Paul's hand. He wagged his tail at Mr. Yamada and licked Grace's fingers.

He'd miss this kind family. They were together now, and safe. Soon, Ben would be well enough to go home. It was time for Ranger to go home, too.

Ranger turned away and found his first aid kit where it had fallen from the cart. It was humming more loudly now. Ranger lowered his head and nuzzled the leather strap around his neck. Light spilled from the cracks in the old metal box, and it grew warm at his throat. The humming got louder and louder, until it drowned out all the hospital cries and street noise. The light grew so bright that Ranger had to close his eyes. He felt as if he were being squeezed through a hole in the sky.

When the humming finally stopped, Ranger opened his eyes.

And saw Luke in the mudroom, eating a Christmas cookie.

Chapter 15

THE TASTE OF HOME

Ranger lowered his head and let the old first aid kit drop onto his dog bed.

"You're missing cookies and carols!" Luke said. He held up a string of popcorn. "And we're doing your favorite part of the decorations."

Luke patted Ranger on the head. Then he noticed the paper tucked under his collar. "Hey, what's this?" Luke pulled out the worn card and started reading.

"'Little Boy kneels at the foot of the bed,'" he read. "Hey! This is a poem from that book

Mom and Dad gave me when I was little!" He read on. "'Droops on the little hands little gold head . . .'"

"I know that one!" Sadie said as she danced into the room. "'Hush! Hush! Whisper who dares! Christopher Robin is saying his prayers.'" She took a dramatic bow, and Luke laughed.

Ranger nuzzled Luke's fingers until Luke handed the paper back to him. "Here you go, boy. I don't know where you found this, but it's all yours."

Ranger took the poem in his teeth and walked to his dog bed. He pawed his blanket aside until he found the treasures he'd brought back from the other times the old first aid kit had sent him to help people. There was a folded-up paper with important words on it, from a different soldier on a faraway beach. There was a bright yellow feather from a girl who had needed Ranger's help to escape from a burning city, and a funny-shaped leaf from the boy he'd met in a big arena full of lions and noise. Those children were all home now.

Somehow, Ranger knew that Ben and Paul and Grace were safe, too. He dropped the poem paper onto his dog bed and pawed at his blanket until it was covered up.

"Come see the tree, Ranger!" Sadie said, heading for the living room.

"It's all lit up now," Luke said, "and there are cookies."

Ranger followed Luke and Sadie into the living room. Mom and Dad were on the couch with a plate of cookies in front of them on the table. Ranger curled up at their feet. Luke plopped down on the floor, cuddled up next to him, and reached for another cookie. He broke off a piece and gave it to Ranger. It was sugary and crumbly and good.

Ranger looked at the twinkling lights and snuggled in beside Luke. He'd miss Ben's gentle hand on his head, Paul's quiet courage, and Grace's kind voice. But his work was done. There were cookies to share. And he was so happy to be home.

AUTHOR'S NOTE:

Ben Hansen and the Yamada family are fictional characters, but they were inspired by the stories of many real people who lived through the bombing of Pearl Harbor on December 7, 1941. The rumors of a possible attack that the characters heard really were swirling around Pearl Harbor in the days leading up to the bombings.

World War II had actually started two years earlier. In September 1939, Germany invaded Poland. Two days later, France and England declared war on Germany. In the spring of 1940, Germany sent troops into Denmark, Norway, the Netherlands, Belgium, and France. In June, Italy jumped into the conflict, and joined Germany in declaring war on Britain and France.

At the same time, Japan was also trying to expand its empire, invading areas of southeast Asia called Indochina and Indonesia. Japan signed an agreement called the Tripartite Pact, along with Italy and Germany. Those three countries promised that if any of them were attacked, the others would come to their defense.

US president Franklin Delano Roosevelt was troubled by all of this. But he also understood that most Americans had no interest in joining the war.

By early 1941, there were whispers that Japan might try to attack America at Pearl Harbor. That January, Navy Secretary Frank Knox sent a letter to Pearl Harbor command. "If war eventuates with Japan," the letter read, "it is believed easily possible that hostilities would be initiated by a surprise attack upon the Fleet or the Naval Base at Pearl Harbor." The letter went on to suggest that those stationed there take every step to prepare for that possibility. They did that, but it wasn't enough.

On the night before the attack, there really was a Battle of Music with the ships' bands. A little girl really did dance with a sailor to win the jitterbug contest that night. That ten-year-old girl was Patricia Campbell, and the sailor was seventeen-year-old Jack Evans from the USS *Tennessee*. Their jitterbug contest trophy is on display at the Pearl Harbor Visitor Center.

The morning after their dance, everything would change. A Japanese aircraft carrier had crossed the ocean undetected and moved into place to stage an attack on Pearl Harbor. The

Pat Campbell

PROGRAM
NAVY RECREATION

BATTLE OF MUSIC
1941

first wave of planes took off from the carrier before sunrise on December 7. Less than two hours later, they arrived at Pearl Harbor, and the raid began. The Japanese planes dropped bombs and torpedoes that devastated the American battleships and nearby Hickam Field on Ford Island. Just after eight o'clock that morning, a bomb hit the USS *Arizona* and destroyed its forward magazine, where the ship's ammunition was stored. It exploded, killing nearly a thousand men.

Ben Hansen's story was inspired by oral histories from several survivors of the *Arizona*, including Master Chief Glen Harvey Lane, who was on board when the bomb hit. Like Ben, he was blasted from the ship and ended up in the oil-covered sea. Lane was rescued by fellow sailors and ended up on another ship, the *Nevada*, which was also under attack. He survived — and went on to spend another thirty years in the military. When Lane died in 2011, his ashes were interred on the sunken ship — an honor offered to survivors of the USS *Arizona* so they can share the final resting place of so many of their friends who died in the attack. If you visit Pearl Harbor today, you can see the memorial that's been built over the remains of the ship to honor them.

When I was doing research for this book, I relied on the stories told by American servicemen and others in Hawaii who lived through the attack. Many of these stories have been archived as oral histories by the National Park Service. I was also fortunate enough to spend some time with Pearl Harbor survivor Everett Hyland when I visited the memorial in December 2018. He served on the battleship USS *Pennsylvania* and was wounded when a bomb exploded not far from his battle station on the morning of December 7, 1941. After nine months of recovery, he returned to military service. When he retired, he became a science teacher and also spent time volunteering at the USS *Arizona* Memorial, telling his story.

I'm grateful for the time Mr. Hyland spent talking with me during my visit. National Park Service volunteer James Lee was also most helpful in sharing his recollections of December 7, 1941. Lee was eleven years old and remembers sitting on the railroad tracks near his home, watching the planes that morning. Like many others, at first, he thought it was a drill and didn't realize it was an attack that would lead to the United States entering World War II.

The attack on Pearl Harbor happened in two waves that morning. By the time it was over, 2,403 Americans had been killed and another 1,178 wounded. The bombings sank or seriously damaged eighteen ships and more than three hundred planes.

The casualties included people who lived in Honolulu as well as members of the military. Some of the American antiaircraft shells being fired at the Japanese planes fell on the city instead. There were explosions all over Honolulu, and many buildings were destroyed or damaged.

The morning of December 7 was only the beginning of the trouble for Japanese Americans who lived in Hawaii. Many were questioned or arrested, suspected of being Japanese spies, even though they were American citizens who had lived in Hawaii their whole lives. In February 1942, President Roosevelt issued an order to send more than 100,000 Japanese Americans to prison camps. These were temporary prisons where people were held, even though most of them had been born in America. These Japanese families spent an average of three years imprisoned before being released. Despite this unfair treatment, more than 30,000 Japanese American men chose to enlist in the US Army and served with distinction during the war. Many were part of a segregated unit called the 442nd Regimental

Combat Team. After the war, President Truman honored those Japanese American veterans with a special ceremony at the White House. "You fought not only the enemy," Truman said, "but you fought prejudice — and you have won."

Yet it would be many more years before America apologized for the way the nation treated Japanese Americans at the start of the war. Finally, in 1988, President Reagan signed a law to compensate more than 100,000 people who were sent to the prison camps. He called it "a policy motivated by racial prejudice, wartime hysteria, and a failure of political leadership."

FURTHER READING:

If you ever have the opportunity to visit the Pearl Harbor National Memorial on the Hawaiian island of Oahu, you should jump at the chance. The site includes not only the USS *Arizona* Memorial but also an extensive visitor center with displays about everything from the years leading up to the attack, through the morning of December 7, 1941, and the months that followed. Nearby are several related sites with more to see and learn about World War II — the Battleship *Missouri* Memorial, the USS *Bowfin* Submarine Museum & Park, and the Pearl Harbor Aviation Museum.

The Pearl Harbor National Memorial also has an excellent website. Many of the Pearl Harbor oral histories collected by the National

Park Service are available at https://www.nps.gov/valr/learn/historyculture/stories.htm.

Here are some other books and websites you might find interesting if you'd like to learn more about Pearl Harbor, the treatment of Japanese Americans during World War II, and working dogs like Ranger:

Baseball Saved Us by Ken Mochizuki, illustrated by Dom Lee (Lee & Low Books, 1993).

Farewell to Manzanar by Jeanne Wakatsuki Houston (Houghton Mifflin Harcourt, 2002).

I Survived the Bombing of Pearl Harbor, 1941 by Lauren Tarshis (Scholastic, 2011).

"Attack on Pearl Harbor" from National Geographic Kids: https://kids.nationalgeographic.com/explore/history/pearl-harbor.

Remember Pearl Harbor: American and Japanese Survivors Tell Their Stories by Thomas B. Allen (National Geographic, 2015).

Sniffer Dogs: How Dogs (and Their Noses) Save the World by Nancy Castaldo (Houghton Mifflin Harcourt, 2014).

What Was Pearl Harbor? by Patricia Brennan Demuth (Penguin Workshop, 2013).

SOURCES:

I'm grateful to the staff and volunteers at the Pearl Harbor National Memorial, especially Everett Hyland and James Lee, for answering my many questions and sharing their stories, and to my friend and fellow author Debbi Michiko Florence, for serving as an early reader for this book. The following sources were also most helpful:

Clarke, Thurston. *Pearl Harbor Ghosts: The Legacy of December 7, 1941*. New York: Ballantine Books, 1991.

Hyland, Everett. Personal Interview. 23 December, 2018.

Jasper, Joy Waldron, James P. Delgado, and Jim Adams. *The USS* Arizona: *The Ship, the Men, the Pearl Harbor Attack, and the Symbol*

That Aroused America. New York: St. Martin's Press, 2001.

Jones, Meg. "75 Years Later, USS *Arizona* Band Remembered." *Milwaukee Journal Sentinel*, December 6, 2016. https://www.jsonline.com/story/news/special-reports/pearl-harbor/2016/12/06/75-years-later-uss-arizona-band-remembered/94626818.

Lee, James. Personal Interview. 23 December, 2018.

The Editors of LIFE. *Pearl Harbor 75 Years Later: A Day of Infamy and Its Legacy*. New York: Liberty Street, 2016.

McWilliams, Bill. *Sunday in Hell: Pearl Harbor Minute by Minute*. New York: Open Road, 2011.

National Park Service Pearl Harbor National Memorial. Oral Histories: https://www.nps.gov/valr/learn/historyculture/oral-history-interviews.htm:

A. H. Mortensen, USS *Oklahoma*

Albert Luco Fickel, USS *Pennsylvania*

Amy Kimura

Bill Guerin, USS *Arizona*

C. E. Thompson, Assistant Fire Chief at Navy Yard

Clinton Westbrook, USS *Arizona*

Donald Stratton, USS *Arizona*

Etsuo Sayama, Kapalama Heights, Oahu

Glen Lane, USS *Arizona*

Harriet Kuwamoto, Kaimuki, Oahu

Harry Goda

Jim Green, USS *Arizona*

Jim Miller, USS *Arizona*

John Anderson, USS *Arizona*

John David Harris, USS *Arizona*

John Evans, USS *Arizona*

John Harry "Jack" McCarron, USS *Arizona*

Loraine Yamada, Honolulu, Oahu

Masao Asada, Kailua, Oahu

Michael M. Ganitch, USS *Pennsylvania*

Milton Tom Hurst, USS *Arizona*

Ruth Yamaguchi, Pearl City, Oahu

Ralph William Landreth, USS *Arizona*

Pearl Harbor Visitors Bureau. "USS *Pennsylvania*: The Day the Music Died." https://visitpearlharbor.org/uss-pennsylvania -day-music-died.

Stratton, Donald, and Ken Gire. *All the Gallant Men: The First Memoir by a USS* Arizona *Survivor.* New York: William Morrow, 2016.

Twomey, Steve. *Countdown to Pearl Harbor: The Twelve Days to the Attack.* New York: Simon & Schuster, 2016.

ABOUT THE AUTHOR

Kate Messner is the author of *Breakout*; *The Seventh Wish*; *All the Answers*; *The Brilliant Fall of Gianna Z.*, recipient of the E.B. White Read Aloud Award for Older Readers; *Capture the Flag*, a *New York Times* Notable Children's Book; and the Ranger in Time and Marty McGuire chapter book series. A former middle-school English teacher, Kate lives on Lake Champlain with her family and loves reading, walking in the woods, and traveling. Visit her online at katemessner.com.

DON'T MISS RANGER'S FIRST ADVENTURE!

He's a golden retriever who has been trained as a search-and-rescue dog but can't officially pass the test because he's always getting distracted by squirrels during exercises. One day, he finds a mysterious first aid kit in the garden and is transported to the year 1850, where he meets a young boy named Sam Abbott. Sam's family is heading west on the Oregon Trail, which can be dangerous. It's up to Ranger to make sure the Abbotts get to Oregon safely! Turn the page for a sneak peek!

Sam Abbott lugged another sack of bacon to the wagon and sat down to wipe his forehead.

"Two more to go!" Pa swung the bacon into place beside a barrel of flour. "Mr. Palmer says we need seventy-five pounds for each adult."

"Too bad Mr. Palmer isn't here to help us carry it," Sam said.

Mr. Palmer had written the guidebook their father held as close as the Bible these days. It told the story of his trip to the Oregon Territory and gave suggestions for how other folks could make the same journey to the fresh air and rich farmland of the Willamette Valley. Most, like Sam's family, traveled to Independence, Missouri, or one of the other jumping-off points first. There, they could get supplies and meet up with a wagon train. Traveling together was safer. For each adult on the journey, Mr. Palmer said to pack:

200 pounds of flour

75 pounds of bacon

30 pounds of pilot bread

10 pounds of rice

Sam and his father had packed some of that before the family set out from their farm near Boonville, Missouri, six days ago. When they arrived in Independence, they'd purchased the rest at a busy trading post. Now they had to finish loading it into the wagon.

Sam's arms ached. How was he going to make it two thousand miles to Oregon when he was already tuckered out just from loading supplies?

M ET RANG

A time-traveling golden retriever with search-and-rescue training... and a nose for danger!

SCHOLASTIC
scholastic.com

RANGER11